P9-CCS-602

Donald Says

Thumbs Down

by Nancy Evans Cooney • pictures by Maxie Chambliss

G. P. Putnam's Sons • New York

To John—N.E.C.

For my John too—MAX

Published simultaneously in Canada
by General Publishing Co. Limited, Toronto.
Printed in Hong Kong by South China Printing Co.

Library of Congress Cataloging-in Publication Data
Cooney, Nancy Evans. Donald says thumbs down.
Summary: Although at first it is very difficult for him to
stop sucking his thumb, Donald gradually substitutes
other activities until he never even thinks
about it any more. [1. Finger-sucking
—Fiction] I. Chambliss, Maxie, ill.
II. Title. PZ7.C7843Do 1987 [E]
86-8189 ISBN 0-399-21373-2
First impression

Donald was truly growing up.

He could pull on his jeans and put his shirt on right side out. He could even fasten his sneakers.

He could eat his dinner without getting any peas on the floor.

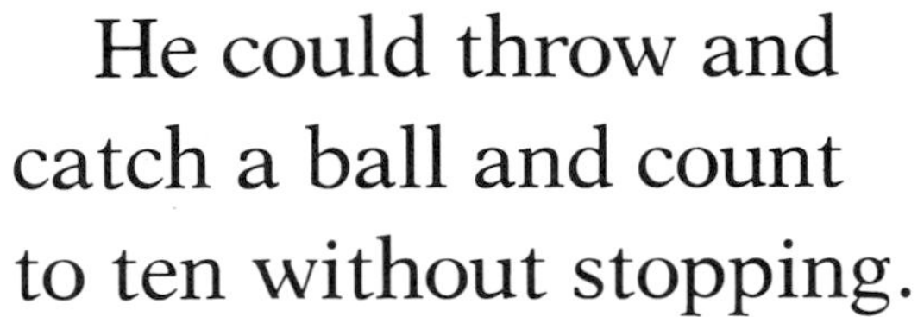

He could throw and catch a ball and count to ten without stopping.

He was lots bigger than his baby sister and much smarter than his dog.

But there were times when Donald was unhappy or tired. And then his left thumb popped into his mouth.

After a while his thumb would become all wrinkled and crinkly and the flavor would be gone, like old gum that was chewed too long. Then he would try his right thumb. But somehow that thumb was not the same.

At nursery school one day, when he was sure no one could see him hiding in the tunnel, Nina found him with his thumb in his mouth and laughed.

Another time, when a ball hit his thumb and he popped it into his mouth, George said, "I *used* to suck my thumb."

Donald began to think he was too big to suck his thumb. He told his father, "I'm going to stop sucking my thumb."

"If that's what you want, fine. But don't worry about it," his father said. "You'll stop sucking your thumb when you're ready to."

Receipt
EBE
ALICE
Paint
FEHLINGE
MISS SARAH sprayer
MAX
FRUIT
Paul Rickert & sons
POTTING SOIL
DAVIS B
Champagne
WONDER GL
PAINT
DURO-
MORGAN
PAK
THE BEST
VICTORIA
ORANGES
by Nanette inc
FEDER
J. J.
GLOSS
JOHN

Donald decided he was ready. And so he tried to stop.

On Tuesday he wore his mittens, but they were too stuffy and itchy and awkward.

On Wednesday he stuck his thumb in his beets at dinner. That made his thumb taste bad. But it was messy.

On Thursday in school he sat on his hands. But that was lumpy and uncomfortable and he couldn't finger-paint.

It was hard not to suck his thumb.

On Friday Donald fell in the playground. He wasn't really hurt, but sucking his thumb helped him feel better. Until Billy pointed at him.

Donald felt awful.

When he told his mother what had happened, she sat right down and pulled him on her lap.

"I'm sorry Billy made you sad. Whenever you feel upset you just come straight to me or Dad. Okay?"

Donald nodded.

Then his mother said, "Let's play a little game. How about Simon Says?"

Donald jumped to the floor and said, "No, let's play *Donald* Says."

"All right," his mother laughed.

He announced, "Donald Says: 'Let's bake cookies.'"

So they did.

After that he ran to his mother each time he was really unhappy. She always stopped whatever she was doing as soon as she could and they snuggled awhile.

Then they would play Donald Says.
Sometimes they all took a walk
through the park,

or played with his
finger puppets,

or painted the toy chest
his father had built,

or puzzled a jigsaw,

or read a book together
while Donald turned
the pages.
Whatever Donald said.

Then one night, as his mother dried him after his bath she said, "You haven't sucked your thumb for days and days."

"I know," Donald whispered. "I still do at night, though."

"Never mind that. I'm really proud of you," and she hugged him tight as she dried his hair with a towel.

Before he got into bed, Donald thought of the long list of things he could do now. He was pleased. And he added, I can go *every* day without sucking my thumb.

He stood in front of his mirror. He stood as tall and as straight as he could, looked himself in the eye and declared: "Donald Says: 'Thumbs down!'"

From that night on, whenever Donald felt like sucking his thumb, he'd hold it up and say to himself, "Donald Says: 'Thumbs down!'" And then he'd do something else instead.

Sometimes he sang. Sometimes he hugged his stuffed monkey.

Sometimes he made shadow puppets on the wall. But he always kept his thumb away from his mouth.

And slowly, very slowly, Donald forgot about sucking his thumb.

Until finally he didn't think about it at all.